# BELLA'S
# DEN

This story first appeared in Muck and Magic ed. Michael Morpurgo,
published in Great Britain 1995 by William Heinemann and Mammoth.
The story has been revised for the Yellow Banana series.

Bella's Den published in Great Britain 1997 by Heinemann and Mammoth,
imprints of Reed International Books Ltd
Michelin House, 81 Fulham Rd, London, SW3 6RB
and Auckland and Melbourne

10 9 8 7 6 5 4 3 2 1

Text copyright © Berlie Doherty 1997
Illustrations copyright © Peter Melnyczuk 1997

The author has asserted her moral rights
The illustrator has asserted his moral rights

Paperback ISBN 0 7497 3113 3
Hardback ISBN 0 434 97469 2

A CIP catalogue record for this title is available
from the British Library

Printed and bound in China

BERLIE DOHERTY

# BELLA'S DEN

Illustrated by
Peter Melnyzcuk

YELLOW BANANAS

*For the Hardy Family*

# Chapter One

WE ALWAYS CAME down the lane on our horses. We galloped faster and faster, mud flying round us, with Polly the sheepdog leaping behind. We had to rein the horses in really hard when we got to the farm gate in case they tried to leap over and sent us flying. Then we tethered them to the fence. Bella's was called Lightning and mine was called Splash. We had to leave them at the fence because they'd never make it through the next bit. They weren't really horses, you see. They were bikes.

I'd been playing horses with Bella for
weeks before she told me about the next bit.
She'd never told anyone else about it, and she
had to get to know me pretty well before she
told me. I had millions of friends where I
lived before, all in my street, and all the way
down town to school. But here there was
only one person to play with for miles, and
that was Bella. And Polly, but you couldn't
count on her because she wasn't even
allowed out with us at lambing time. So it
was a good job I got on with Bella.

I didn't always, though. She had an
annoying habit of disappearing. Sometimes, if
we had an argument about whose horse had
won or whose turn it was to close the farm
gate, she would just stand there with her face
closing up as if she was thinking, 'I don't
have to play with you, you know.' I'd go back
to shut the gate and she'd disappear. I just
didn't know how she did it. Polly went too. It
was no use waiting for them or shouting their
names. I'd just have to wheel my horse back

home and sit watching telly, like I used to do
when we first came here. She had a secret,
Bella had, and she was pretty good at
keeping it.

Then one day she seemed to make up her mind about me. It was her turn to shut the farm gate and I said, 'Bella, I wish you'd tell me where you go when you disappear.' And she did.

## Chapter Two

THIS IS WHAT you do.

You stand by the fence just where there's a patch that's always muddy. You can tell where the barbed wire has been stretched. You look both ways, up and down the lane. Then you duck under the wire and slither down a really steep slope. It's no good clinging onto plants or branches because they'd only come away with you. But if you look carefully you can just make out Bella's path, a thin zig-zaggy line like the tracks that sheep and rabbits make.

You have to roll
down the last bit,
there's no other
way, and you
have to jump up
sharp because
you've come to
the river then.
It isn't very
wide just there
so it's easy to leap
across it, but I advise you to wear

wellies anyway.

Now you're on a little
bare hill with holes in it.
You scramble up this and
duck under some
branches and there it is.

'There,' says Bella.
'My den.'

The roots of a tree jut
out like a shelf, and
underneath them it is

hollow. There are strands of grass and moss trailing over it, and when you lift them up there's a bit of an old ladder, and part of a crate making a door. There's a sheep's skull nailed onto the door with some teeth missing and half a horn broken off. You crawl in through the door and pull the grasses down. It's dark and damp and it smells of earth. It smells a million years old.

And there you are, huddled right in so nobody can see you. But you can see out. It's so quiet. All you can hear is the river, like a long, long sigh.

'I bet nobody ever comes here,' I whisper.

'Nobody knows about it,' Bella whispers back. 'Except me.'

And me now.

But that's not all.

If you scramble out and look round in the bed of mosses by the hill you can see there's a loose tufty bit that's not attached to anything. Lift it up and you've found the treasure trove. There are pieces of crockery with lovely patterns. Some of them have gold on too. And there's a Santa Claus brooch with a bent pin.

That's still not all. There are pools around here that nobody would find even if they came searching for them. There's Midge Pool and the Bog of Eternal Stench, Rowan Hole and Stinkweed Bog (that's where we empty out our cups of nettle tea). Over there in the leaf bed is where the hedgehogs sleep. They'll be there till spring. And there's Minibeast House, where we put all the insects and bugs that need looking after.

And that's still not all. Underneath the bare
mound there's a patch that's all peaty and
black, and at one time nothing grew there at
all. But do you see those trees? Twigs really,
you might think, but they're growing, they
really are.

'They're twice as big as they were when
we put them in last year,' Bella tells me.

'We?'

'Tom and Jessica.'

I can't tell you how jealous I feel then. This is our den. It belongs to me and Bella. I've never even heard of Tom and Jessica. 'You said you hadn't told anyone else about it,' I say. I feel like pulling up those twigs.

'I found it at the same time as they did. We were together,' Bella says. 'So how could I have told them about it? We planted the trees the day they left, ages before you came. One each.'

'Don't they come any more?' I am beginning to feel a bit better.

'Of course they don't. They live miles and miles away now. Nobody comes here, I told you. Except me. I come every now and again to tidy up a bit. I'm looking after it. But it's not as good, on my own.'

# Chapter Three

IT WAS A LONG time before I went back to
the den. Bella didn't invite me, and I didn't
really feel I should go there without her. I
told myself it was a silly sort of place to go
anyway. I missed my friends. We never
needed a den where I used to live. But once
Bella had shown me its real secret, its deep-
down dark secret, I knew for sure that it was
the most special place in the world, and that
it was just as much mine as Bella's.

It was a kind of dare at first. A challenge.
Bella was staying at my house for the night

because her mum and dad were going to be
out late. We persuaded my mum to let us
sleep out in the garden in Bella's tent. There
really is a little campsite out in the field
behind the cottages, but that belongs to the
farm. I like to watch the campers sometimes,
especially at night, when their tents glow like
coloured moons on the grass. We didn't have
a torch or a lamp in our tent. You don't need
one really, especially when the moon is as
full as it was that night.

We couldn't sleep because
the tawny owls were having
a conversation, one in
each tree in the garden.
They sounded like
people with really bad
colds sneezing their
heads off. First one
would sneeze out,
making you jump out
of your skin, and then
you'd be just about to
drift off to sleep when
another one would
answer. They kept this
up for over an hour and
I was all for climbing up
the trees and scaring
them off.

Bella squirmed out of
her sleeping bag and
started pulling on
her wellies.

'Where are you going?' I asked.

'The den, of course.'

'Now?'

But she was off before I had a chance to discuss it with her. You don't actually discuss things with Bella. But it took me exactly five seconds to make up my mind. If Bella could do it, then so could I.

I draped my sleeping bag round my shoulders like a cloak, stuck my bare feet in my wellies and grabbed the packet of ginger nuts. By this time Bella was out of sight. The horses were in the garage and it would have made too much noise to get them out, so I flopped through the farmyard after her till I'd worked my feet properly into the wellies, ran over the bridge

14

and up the lane and searched in the
moonlight for the muddy patch. I heard my
sleeping bag rip a bit on the barbed wire and
reminded myself to look for any torn bits on
the fence next day. It would never do for us
to leave tracks behind us.

Then I lost my footing and slid all the
way down the bank. I'm proud to say I
didn't yell out. My sleeping bag finally
fell off when I was crossing the river,
and I stung myself on some nettles
as I was trying to rescue it. But it
was all worth it, every inch
of agony was worth it,
because of what
happened next.

# Chapter Four

WE MUST HAVE been in the den for nearly an hour. There wasn't room for us both to lie down so we were sitting crouched together with Bella's sleeping bag pulled across us both. We were both staring out into the night. It was so dark then that it didn't seem to have any depth. It was like a black curtain, just too far away to reach out and touch.

Then the moon slid away from the clouds and shone through the trailing leaves covering the den. It was suddenly as clear as day. And I think I was the first to see it. I was looking

at the big mound below the
den, and thinking how the
moonlight made it look
like a theatre with the
stage lights on, and how
deep and black those holes were,
when I caught sight of a movement. I touched
Bella's arm and she let out a little breath of,
yes, she'd seen it too.

It was a fox. He seemed to grow out of the
darkness of the hole, and then took shape as
the moon lit him. He stood as if he had been
turned to stone, and he was
staring right at our den,
right through the
leaf strands, right
at me. He was
locked right
into me,
reading the
thoughts in
my mind, and I
daren't move or

17

breathe, I daren't do anything but stare back at him, till my eyes were blurring. I thought I would pass out with holding myself so still, and my skin was ice-cold, frozen cold with fear.

Then all of a sudden he seemed to relax. He turned his head slightly, and, as if it was a signal of some sort, out came another fox and three little cubs, four shapes looming out of the hole, each one faster than the one before. They were bouncing out like infants in a school playground, tumbling red and brown and silvery white.

The dog fox slunk off into the shadows.
The other biggish fox, his vixen, sat just
where he had been, just at the mouth of the
hole. She pricked up her ears and her head
turned from time to time as she listened
out for all kinds of sounds in the hills.

But the three cubs had come out to play. They cuffed each other and fell over and rolled about, jumped on each other, jumped on her, hid from each other and roly-polyed right down to the river. I could hear them breathing, and scuffling with their paws. I could hear the little puffs of sound they made when they biffed each other. It felt as if it was the middle of the world, this little patch of ground where the foxes were playing, as if nothing else that was happening anywhere was as important as this.

I've no idea what the signal was, but the vixen suddenly turned her head, sharp. The cubs scrambled up the bank and one by one slid back inside the hole. She waited a moment, lifted her head slightly then just melted down into the hole after them, sliding like water into it. It went dark again, as if the moon had been put out.

I strained my eyes and I'm not sure whether I really saw it or not, but there seemed to be another shape, like a dark fluttering where

the hole was, and a dull white glow like the
tip of a tail disappearing into it.

## Chapter Five.

NEXT DAY I was full of it. 'I've seen a fox,' I said to my mum. 'A real fox. And all its cubs. Three of them! They were playing!'

We were standing in the farmyard as I was telling her this. Bella had just come running towards me from her cottage, and the farmer came out of the lambing shed at the same time. He stood looking down at me.

'Where did you see this fox?' he asked me.

I waved my arm in the direction of Bella's den, and then I saw the look on her face. I couldn't believe what I'd done.

'Where exactly?' he asked.

I shook my head. 'I don't remember,'
I stammered.

Mum looked at me oddly.

'Vixen and three cubs?' the farmer
asked me again.

I nodded. I couldn't look him in the eyes any more. I couldn't look at my mum. Bella had turned her back on me. The sandy earth was beginning to swirl around me, and I felt sick at heart.

'You know what foxes do, don't you?' the farmer said. 'They bite lambs' heads off!'

Bella started to run back to her cottage. I ran after her. She closed her gate so I couldn't follow her in.

'You're not allowed to go to my den again,' she said. Her voice was like ice. 'Never, never, never.'

I went up to my room, all the joy of last night drained away from me. I wished I could unsay what I'd said. I wished I could say, 'It wasn't true. I didn't really see a fox,' or 'It wasn't over there. It was the other way, over the railway line.' But it was too late.

From my window I could
see sheep grazing, fields
and fields of them. They had
lambs by their sides. Lots of
the lambs were newly born,
with little bendy, bouncy
legs and wagging tails. The
older ones were already
learning to play with each
other. They were bounding
up the little haystacks the
farmer made for them, taking
it in turns to jump off and
running back up the pile.
And in my mind's eye I
could see the dog fox, the
secret fox, slinking off into
the night fields. What would
he feed his cubs on, when
they tumbled back down into
their lair?

Now I would never see
them again.

# Chapter Six.

THAT NIGHT I saw the farmer going down
the lane with his gun across his shoulder. I
ran back into our house and sobbed and
sobbed and Mum held me in her arms and
said, 'It's his business, not ours. He has to
protect his sheep. It's his job.'

But nothing would console me. I didn't
know what to say to Bella. It was the end of
our friendship. There was no more paddling
in the river in our wellies, no more riding
down the lane on Splash and Lightning. I
knew I would never dare go to the den again.

We got on the school bus every morning and sat at different ends of it, just the two of us.

'I wish I didn't live here!' I said to Mum. 'I hate it! I wish we could move.'

'What is it?' asked Mum, worried. 'What is it you don't like about living here?'

I couldn't tell her. It was everything. I'd lost Bella, I'd lost the den, and I'd lost the fox.

One day I plucked up courage to ask the farmer about it. He was always jokey and friendly with us. I couldn't believe that he would shoot foxes, in spite of what Mum said. So I went up to him when he was cleaning out the sheep pens one day. I made a fuss of Meg, the dog, and then I said, 'Joe, do you really shoot foxes?'

He straightened up and looked at me as if I was a bit daft. Then he said, 'I don't kill things for the fun of it, you know. But if they bother my sheep, I do. Yes.'

I didn't know what to make of his answer. I didn't know whether it made me feel better or not.

# Chapter Seven

FUNNY, BUT IT wasn't us who moved. It was Bella and her family. Her father had got a different job, in the Lake District. 'It'll be wonderful for them,' Mum said. 'Even more beautiful than here. But poor Bella! She's broken-hearted about moving. Her mother can't get a smile out of her these days.'

The next day I watched Bella on the bus, and I wished I could say something to her. But she just sat with her head hunched into her shoulders and wouldn't return my look.

On the day they were moving Mum went

down to give Bella's mum
and dad a hand. 'Come
and say goodbye to her,'
she said. 'You used to be
such good friends!'

When we knocked at
the door there was no
one in. Bella's mother
and Polly came running
down the lane towards us.
'I can't find Bella!' she
gasped. She's nowhere
to be found!'

'I'll help,' Mum said.
'Have you tried all the barns?'

They ran off together,
with Polly bounding after
them. But I didn't follow
them. I knew exactly
where Bella would be.

I ran down the lane, through the gate, and up to the fence by the muddy patch. I looked both ways, up and down the lane. Then I ducked under the wire and slithered down the slope, as close to the thin zig-zaggy track as I could. I rolled down the last bit, and jumped up sharp when I came to the river. I leaped across it. Now I was on the little bare hill with holes in it. I scrambled up it and ducked under the branches and there it was. Bella's den.

'Bella?' I called.

I could hear her sniffing behind the curtain of grass.

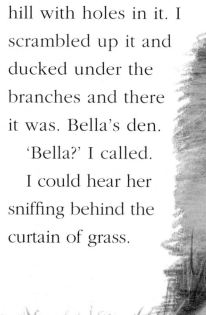

I sat just outside it. I didn't know what to say to her. But I didn't want to leave her. It was really hot. There were swallows darting just above the river, catching insects. Miles above me I could hear a skylark singing. It was too tiny to see.

'I'm sorry you're going, Bella,' I said.

She sniffed.

'I'd hate to have to leave here,' I said.

Another sniff.

'And I'm . . . I'm sorry about the foxes.' There, I'd said it at last. After all those weeks.

'The foxes?'

Just as she said that,

the air seemed to go silent. I felt something
rippling down the back of my neck, as if the
hairs were standing on end. Have you ever
had that feeling that you were being watched?
I turned my head, very slowly, and there it
was looking at me, looking right into me,
through my eyes and into my head. It was the
fox. We stared at each other. Then it sank
down away from sight and into its lair.

I was so excited that I could hardly breathe.
I wanted to scream with laughter. I wanted to
roll about on the slope that the cubs had
played on all those weeks ago, to tumble
down it and splash into the river and
scramble up again. I wanted to sing louder
than the skylark.

I pulled Bella out of her den and danced round with her. She tried to pull away from me at first and then she started laughing. We were both shrieking with laughter. We swung each other round until we couldn't stay on our feet any longer.

'You're my best friend, Bella!' I shouted.

'You're mine!' she shouted back.

'I won't forget you!' I yelled.

'Never, never, never!' she hollered back.

# Chapter Eight

I OFTEN GO to the den now. I tidy round a bit and look after the trees that are growing here for Tom and Jessica. There's a little twig for Bella too, that we planted together.

When I've tidied round I always go and crawl into the den. I huddle right in so nobody can see me, but I can see out. It's so quiet. All you can hear is the river, like a long, long sigh.

That's when the fox comes out. He always stares at me the same way, looking right through my eyes, right inside my head.

We share each other's secret.

It's so quiet here, you see. There's nothing to scare him away.

I haven't told anyone else about the den. I'm only telling you now because one day, if something happens to stop me from coming here, it will need looking after.

It's very special, you see. Bella's den.

# Have you enjoyed this Yellow Banana? There are plenty more to read. Why not try one of these exciting new stories:

### A Funny sort of Dog *by Elizabeth Laird*
There's something not quite right about Simon's new puppy, Tip. It's very big with long claws, and it roars. Then one day it climbs a tree and Simon has to face the truth . . . perhaps Tip isn't a dog at all!

### Ghostly Guests *by Penelope Lively*
When the Brown family move to a new house, Marion and Simon discover there are three ghosts already living there! The ghosts make their lives unbearable – how can the children get rid of them?

### Carole's Camel *by Michael Hardcastle*
Carole is left a rather unusual present – a camel called Umberto. It's great to ride him to school and everyone loves him, even if he is rather smelly. But looking after a real camel can cause a lot of problems. Perhaps she should find him a more suitable home . . .

### The Pony that went to Sea *by K.M. Peyton*
Paddy, an old forgotten pony, is adopted by Tom and Emily Tarboy. One stormy night, Paddy is taken aboard the houseboat where the children live. But during the night the boat breaks free and is carried out to sea. It's up to Paddy to save the day.

### Ollie and the Trainers *by Rachel Anderson*
Ollie has two problems: he has no trainers and he can't read. Dad agrees to buy him some trainers but they turn out to be no ordinary pair. They are Secret Readers and can talk! Can Leftfoot Peter and Rightfoot Paul help Ollie to read?